THE PIRATE WHO LOST HIS AARRR!

By Marcus Wild &
Crystal J. Stranaghan

FOR ETHAN

Aarrr Matey! I hope ye
like me story xox

gumboot books
www.gumbootbooks.com

THIS BOOK HERE BE THE PROPERTY OF

X _____

" SQWAARK HERE ARE THE RULES OF THE DICE GAME.
ROLL THE DICE AND ADD UP THE DOTS TO DETERMINE
HOW MANY PLACES YOU MOVE ACROSS THE
PIRATE MAP. MOVE YOUR COUNTER AND IF
YOU GET TO THE TREASURE FIRST,
THEN YOU ARE THE WINN*AAAR !* "

For Mo and Bernie Wild, for all their unwavering support, inspiration and love. MW

For my dad, who passed along his love of the sea and taught me how to captain a ship. CJS

HAARRR! HAARRR! HAARRR!

Q: Why do pirates carry a bar of soap?

A: So, if they are ship-wrecked they can wash themselves to shore!

Q: Why didn't the pirate get hungry on the desert island?

A: Because of all the sand which is there!

Q: How much does it cost a pirate to get ear rings?

A: A Buccaneer!

Q: How much did the pirate pay for his peg leg and hook?

A: An arm and a leg!

START

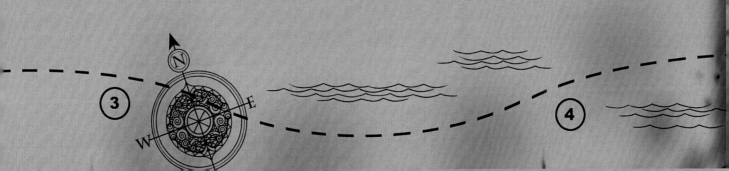

All the local townsfolk—those quite near and those quite far—couldn't help but pay attention when the baby hollered...

ATTACKED BY SEA MONSTER
GO BACK 2 PLACES.

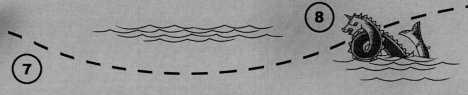

8

His parents hoped that he would be
a lawyer or a sarge,
but all he played was "pirates"
'cause he loved to holler...

As the boy became a man, he had to make a choice.

How exactly would he use the power of his voice?

STRONG WINDS BLOW
YOU ONTO THE NEXT PAGE.

AAAA

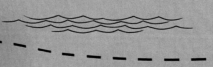

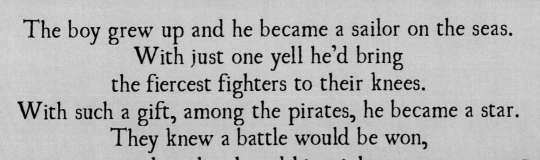

The boy grew up and he became a sailor on the seas.
With just one yell he'd bring
the fiercest fighters to their knees.
With such a gift, among the pirates, he became a star.
They knew a battle would be won,
when they heard his mighty...

ARRRRRR !

MAROONED ON A DESERT
ISLAND, ROLL A 6
TO MOVE ON.

The man became a captain, and his mates were fierce and strong. He often kept them swabbing decks and working all day long.

They grumbled and complained a bit, but Captain's rules were fair. He might make them work hard, but when they won they got a share.

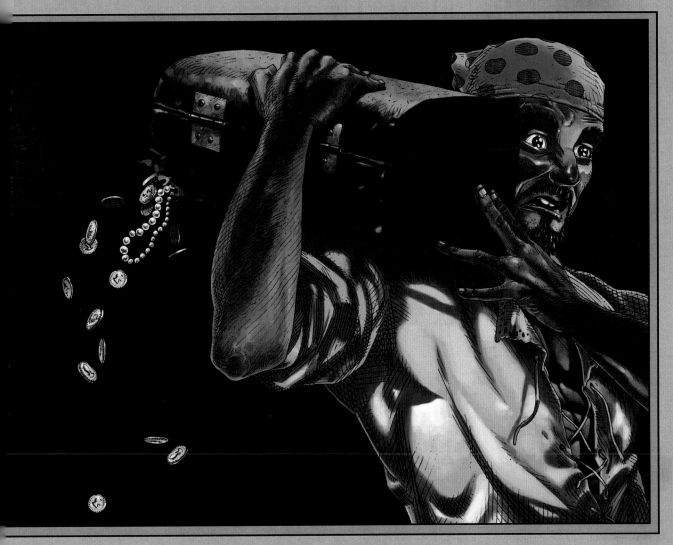

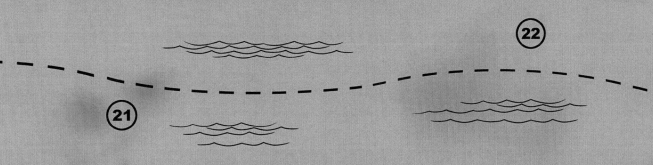

But then a scurvy sailor dropped a chest off the ship's deck.
It wasn't really that much gold, but Captain gave him heck.

STOP TO PICK UP SUPPLIES.
ROLL A 3 TO CONTINUE.

It clearly was an accident.
The pirate felt real bad.
But Captain lost his temper
and got hopping,
flaming, mad!

He may have overdone it though,
and gone a bit too far,
when he let out one almighty
roaring, never ending...

This seemed a tad excessive for one innocent mistake.
To use that voice on his own crew, was more than they could take.
The pirates were upset with him—but all of them kept quiet.
They thought someone should speak to him, but no one dared to try it.

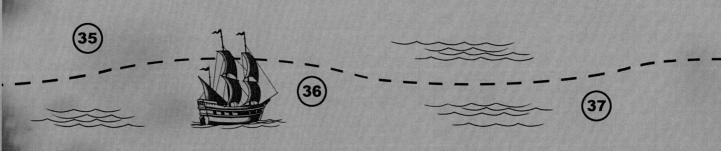

The pirates all were miserable, though some thought that they hid it.
They still did *almost* all their work, but grumbled while they did it.
As they regained their hearing, and they finally stopped shaking,
they noticed something strange about the noises Cap was making.

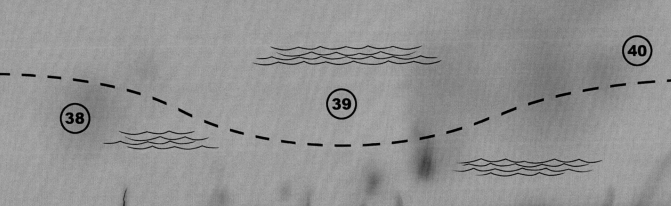

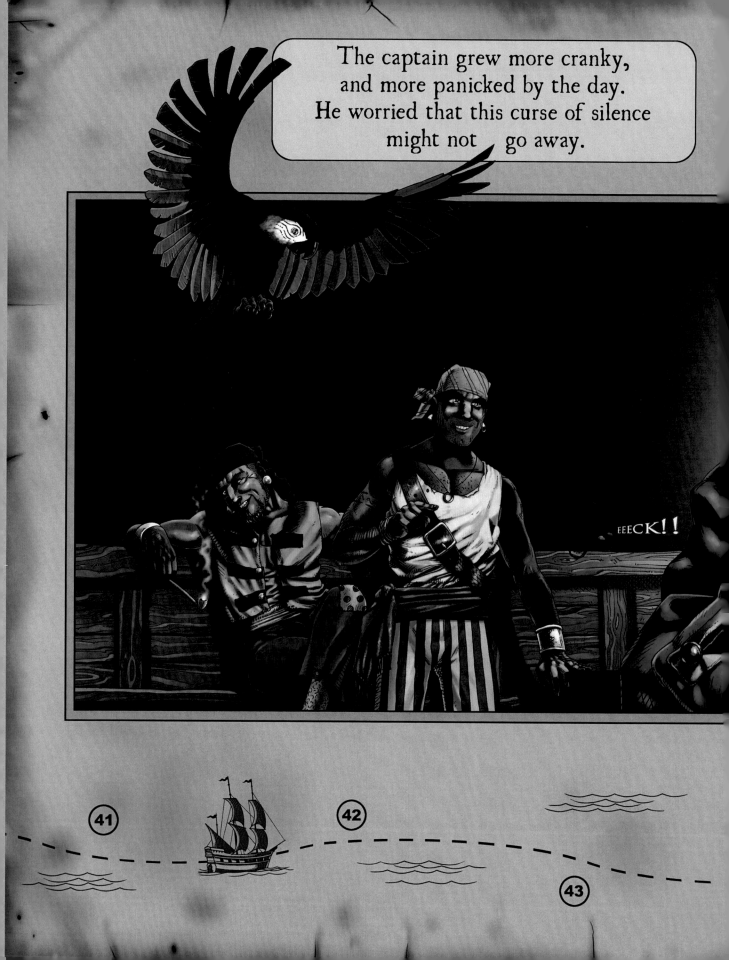

The crew waited for orders, but the captain couldn't speak.
Every time his mouth would open, out would come a squeak!
At first the pirates laughed at him—they thought that it was funny.
Until they realized, no voice for Captain means no money!

FORGED TO WALK THE PLANK.
GO BACK 3 PLACES.

Without the captain's mighty AARRR! a battle could be lost. For just one fit of temper Captain paid a mighty cost. One by one the crew snuck off, until not one remained. But Captain couldn't say a thing, no matter how he strained.

He prayed to every God he knew to give him back his voice.
He hadn't understood a curse could come from one bad choice.
He swore that in the future he would only use his AARRR!
to help out all his pirate mates, and never cause them harm.

He thought maybe a cannon blast would
carry far and wide,
and then his men would hear it
and would stand back by his side.
The cannon boomed, while Captain sat
alone upon the deck.
He waited, but just townsfolk came,
and gave the captain heck.

CHASED OFF COURSE BY THE THE ROYAL NAVY.
GO BACK 2 PLACES.

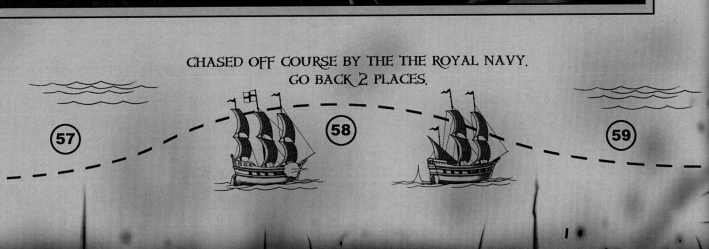

57   58   59

He offered up a gold reward, for
news of his old crew.
But pirates can be hard to find
if they don't want you to.

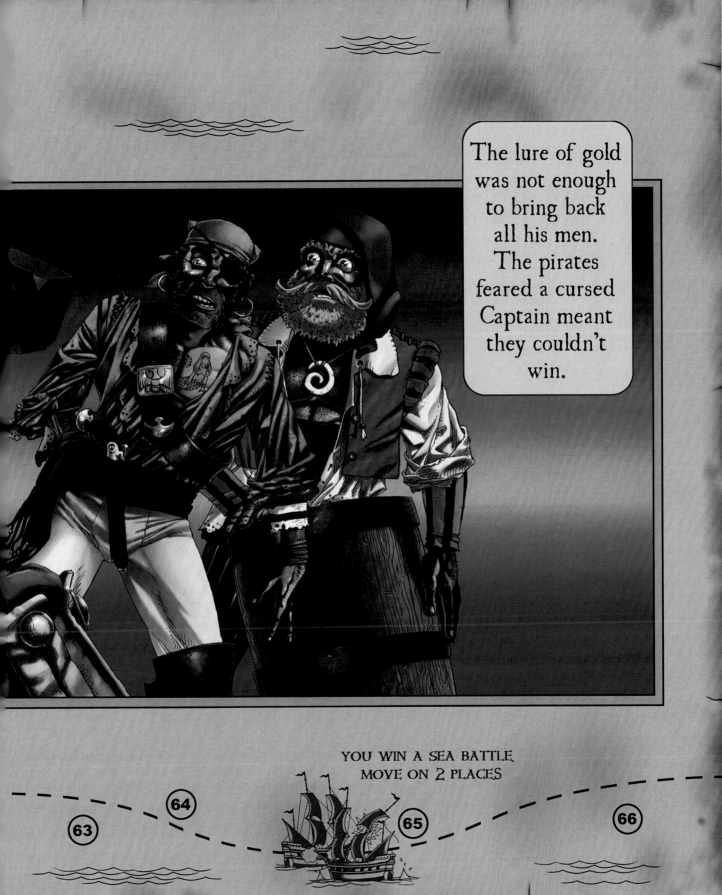

The lure of gold was not enough to bring back all his men. The pirates feared a cursed Captain meant they couldn't win.

YOU WIN A SEA BATTLE.
MOVE ON 2 PLACES

63   64   65   66

He searched the sea for answers but all he could find was space. Nothing much got done as Cap just sailed from place to place.

He wasn't all that good at many of the pirate jobs. Paint was peeling, sails were loose, the decks weren't getting swabbed. The Captain soon grew desperate, but what could just one man do? A captain's not a Captain if he hasn't got a crew.

STRONG WINDS BLOW YOU ON 2 PLACES.

70   71   72

CAUGHT IN A STORM,
GO BACK 2 PLACES.

73   74   75

Captain wished with all his heart that he could take it back.
If he could just go back in time, he'd try a different tack.
Now if a clumsy pirate tripped and dropped a chest of gold,
He'd never AARRR! at his own men—his temper he would hold.

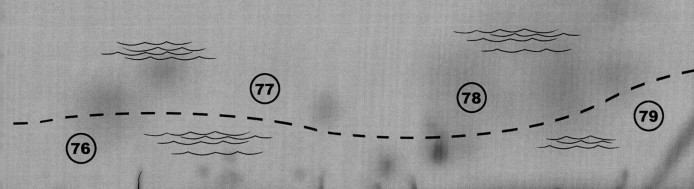

He was upset and hammering—trying to fix a rail,
but the hammer slipped and pounded on his
thumb and not the nail. He really must have wound up
good and hit himself quite hard.

WALLOP !!!

Captain quite surprised himself when he **bellowed** out an...

82

YOU SINK A RIVAL PIRATE SHIP.
MOVE ON 2 PLACES.

83

84

STRUCK BY LIGHTNING.
GO BACK 2 PLACES.

The pirates heard his mighty voice
and all of them did ken,
that maybe it was time to get
back on the sea again.
Convinced if Captain's voice was back,
the curse must have been lifted,
they came from every town and port.
Towards his voice they drifted.

The Captain used his booming voice to give them all a speech, and said he'd learned his lesson while they rested on the beach.

He said if every pirate promised that he'd do his best, then he'd control his temper next time someone dropped a chest. He said that they could make mistakes—they all would get just one. Because he knew, without his shipmates, nothing could get done.

At this, the pirates raised a ruckus, heard both near and far, as the crew rejoined their captain with a

mighty, roaring...

AAAAARRRRRRR!!!

STRANDED ON A SAND BANK
ROLL A 2 TO BRING THE
TIDE BACK IN.

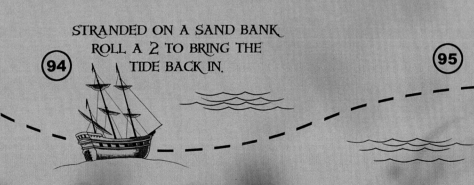

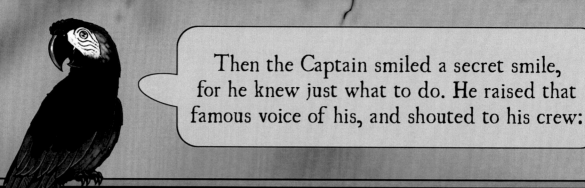

Then the Captain smiled a secret smile, for he knew just what to do. He raised that famous voice of his, and shouted to his crew:

AVAST !
AHOY, YE SCURVY DOGS.
YE'RE LILY-LIVERED, TOO.

NOW HOIST THAT SAIL,
AND CLIMB THE MAST,
YE ALL KNOW WHAT TO DO.

99 SHIPWRECKED ON A REEF. THROW A 6 TO SWIM ASHORE.

98

100 ✗ BURIED TREASURE

ABOUT MARCUS WILD
www.marcuswild.com

Marcus grew up in Wakefield, a city in Yorkshire, England. After graduating from Wolverhampton University with a Degree in Design and Illustration he travelled to London where he worked in an artists' studio as a storyboard artist and illustrator. In 2001 he moved to Vancouver, Canada and found employment as a concept artist for video game companies such as EA Sports and Next Level Games. He has also had 3 exhibitions of his large paintings. This book is his 1st adventure into the field of publishing. He is very grateful to Crystal for helping him create a beautiful book that has been in his mind for a very long time. Hopefully the first of many!

ABOUT CRYSTAL J. STRANAGHAN
www.crystalstranaghan.com

Torn between her fascination with real people and the ones who exist through stories, Crystal's education has been a balancing act between studying English Literature and Psychology. She spent several years as a professional fundraiser for non-profit societies, and traveling around BC doing workshkops on goal-setting, teambuilding and event planning and promotion for student groups. Crystal is the author of several picture books for children, including: *Then it Rained, Vernon and the Snake, The 13th Floor: Primed for Adventure, Faeries Are Real* and "Tontii" in the *World of Stories* collection. When she isn't making books, she enjoys traveling around to schools all over BC teaching people of all ages about writing and making books! Crystal also teaches workshops on self-publishing, leadership, teambuilding and wellness. She lives in Vancouver, Canada with her partner, in life and business, Jared.

English Version
ISBN 978-1-926691-01-5

Note for Librarians
A cataloguing record for this title is available from
Library and Archives Canada at
www.collectionscanada.ca/amicus/index-e.html.

This book printed in Canada
by Island Blue / Printorium Bookworks.

FOR MORE PIRATE FUN, COME VISIT OUR PIRATE CAVE ONLINE AT

WWW.GUMBOOTBOOKS.CA

Gumboot Books is a socially and environmentally responsible company, and we measure our success by the impact we have on the lives and dreams of our authors and illustrators, the impact we have on the environment, and the ways in which we help to enrich the lives of everyone who reads our books.

If you'd like to see how else we are reducing our ecological footprint, and how we are supporting community numeracy and literacy projects, please visit us online.

www.gumbootbooks.com

ORDERING INFORMATION

All of our products are available through Amazon.com, Amazon.ca and other online retailers, directly from Gumboot Books online or call us toll free at 1-888-803-4861 .

Quantity **discounts are available** on bulk purchases of this book for resale, educational purposes, subscription incentives, or fundraising initiatives.

For more information, or to place an order, please visit us online at **www.gumbootbooks.com** or call 1-888-803-4861 (toll-free from anywhere in North America).